RED ROOM ESCAPEE. HANK PYM'S DAUGHTER.
SUPER-SCIENCING FOR GOOD. NADIA IS...

THE UNSTOPPABLE WASP

UNSTOPPABLE! #2

NADIA HAS A NEW MISSION: TO RECRUIT
FEMALE GENIUSES TO HER LAB AND USE
THEIR COMBINED KNOWLEDGE TO CHANGE
THE WORLD FOR THE BETTER. BUT THE
PATH BEFORE HER WON'T BE EASY:
SHE STILL DOESN'T HAVE AMERICAN
CITIZENSHIP, AND THE RUSSIAN RED
ROOM IS EAGER TO RECLAIM THEIR
STAR SCIENTIST.

PLUS, SHE'S GOT A LOT OF DONUTS TO EAT.

writer
JEREMY WHITLEY

artist
ELSA CHARRETIER

color artist
MEGAN WILSON

letterer
VC'S JOE CARAMAGNA

cover
ELSA CHARRETIER & NICOLAS BANNISTER

variant cover
TONY FLEECS

editors
ALANNA SMITH & TOM BREVOORT

editor in chief
AXEL ALONSO

chief creative officer
JOE QUESADA

publisher
DAN BUCKLEY

executive producer
ALAN FINE

SPECIAL THANKS TO PREETI CHHIBBER, MARK WAID AND ALEX ROSS

WASP CREATED BY STAN LEE, ERNIE HART AND JACK KIRBY

MARVEL   ABDO Spotlight

ABDOBOOKS.COM

Reinforced library bound edition published in 2020 by Spotlight,
a division of ABDO, PO Box 398166, Minneapolis, Minnesota 55439.
Spotlight produces high-quality reinforced library bound editions for
schools and libraries. Published by agreement with Marvel Characters, Inc.

Printed in the United States of America, North Mankato, Minnesota.
042019
092019

THIS BOOK CONTAINS
RECYCLED MATERIALS

marvelkids.com
© 2020 MARVEL

Library of Congress Control Number: 2018965979

Publisher's Cataloging-in-Publication Data

Names: Whitley, Jeremy, author. | Charretier, Elsa; Wilson, Megan, illustrators.
Title: Unstoppable! / writer: Jeremy Whitley; art: Elsa Charretier; Megan Wilson.
Description: Minneapolis, Minnesota : Spotlight, 2020 | Series: The unstoppable
    Wasp
Summary: Nadia Pym spreads her wings as she recruits girl geniuses of the Marvel
    universe, battles evil scientists and man-eating rats, and avoids the Red Room's
    clutches.
Identifiers: ISBN 9781532143656 (#1 ; lib. bdg.) | ISBN 9781532143663 (#2 ; lib.
    bdg.) | ISBN 9781532143670 (#3 ; lib. bdg.) | ISBN 9781532143687 (#4 ; lib.
    bdg.)
Subjects: LCSH: Wasp (Fictitious character)--Juvenile fiction. | Superheroes--Juvenile
    fiction. | Women superheroes--Juvenile fiction. | Graphic novels--Juvenile
    fiction. | Geniuses--Juvenile fiction. | Superpowers--Juvenile fiction. | Comic
    books, strips, etc--Juvenile fiction.
Classification: DDC 741.5--dc23

Spotlight

A Division of ABDO
abdobooks.com

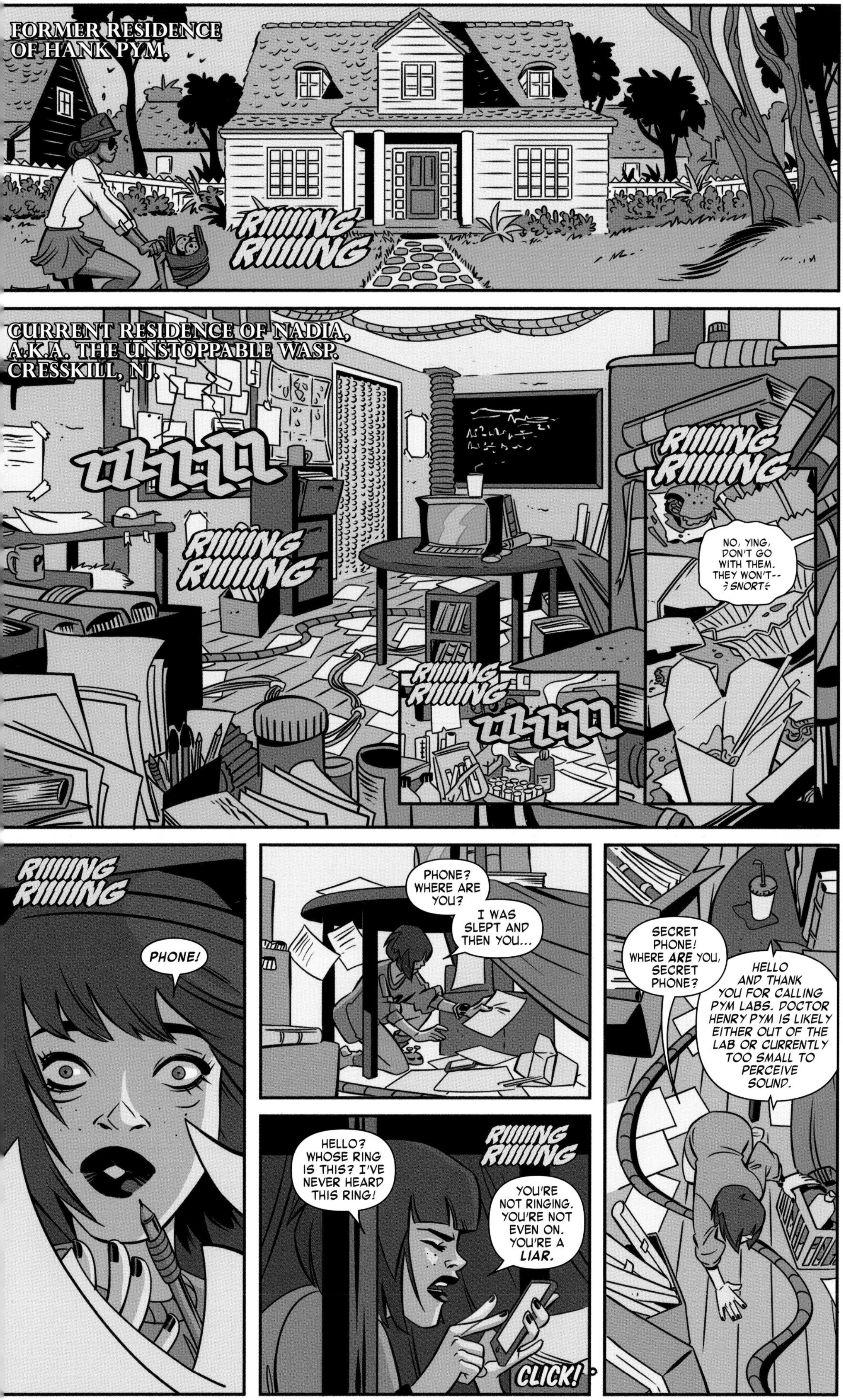
FORMER RESIDENCE OF HANK PYM.
RIIIING RIIIING
CURRENT RESIDENCE OF NADIA, A.K.A. THE UNSTOPPABLE WASP. CRESSKILL, NJ.
ZZZZZ
RIIIING RIIIING
RIIIING RIIIING
NO, YING, DON'T GO WITH THEM. THEY WON'T-- *SNORT*
RIIIING RIIIING
ZZZZZ
RIIIING RIIIING
PHONE!
PHONE? WHERE ARE YOU?
I WAS SLEPT AND THEN YOU...
HELLO? WHOSE RING IS THIS? I'VE NEVER HEARD THIS RING!
RIIIING RIIIING
YOU'RE NOT RINGING. YOU'RE NOT EVEN ON. YOU'RE A LIAR.
CLICK!
SECRET PHONE! WHERE ARE YOU, SECRET PHONE?
HELLO AND THANK YOU FOR CALLING PYM LABS. DOCTOR HENRY PYM IS LIKELY EITHER OUT OF THE LAB OR CURRENTLY TOO SMALL TO PERCEIVE SOUND.

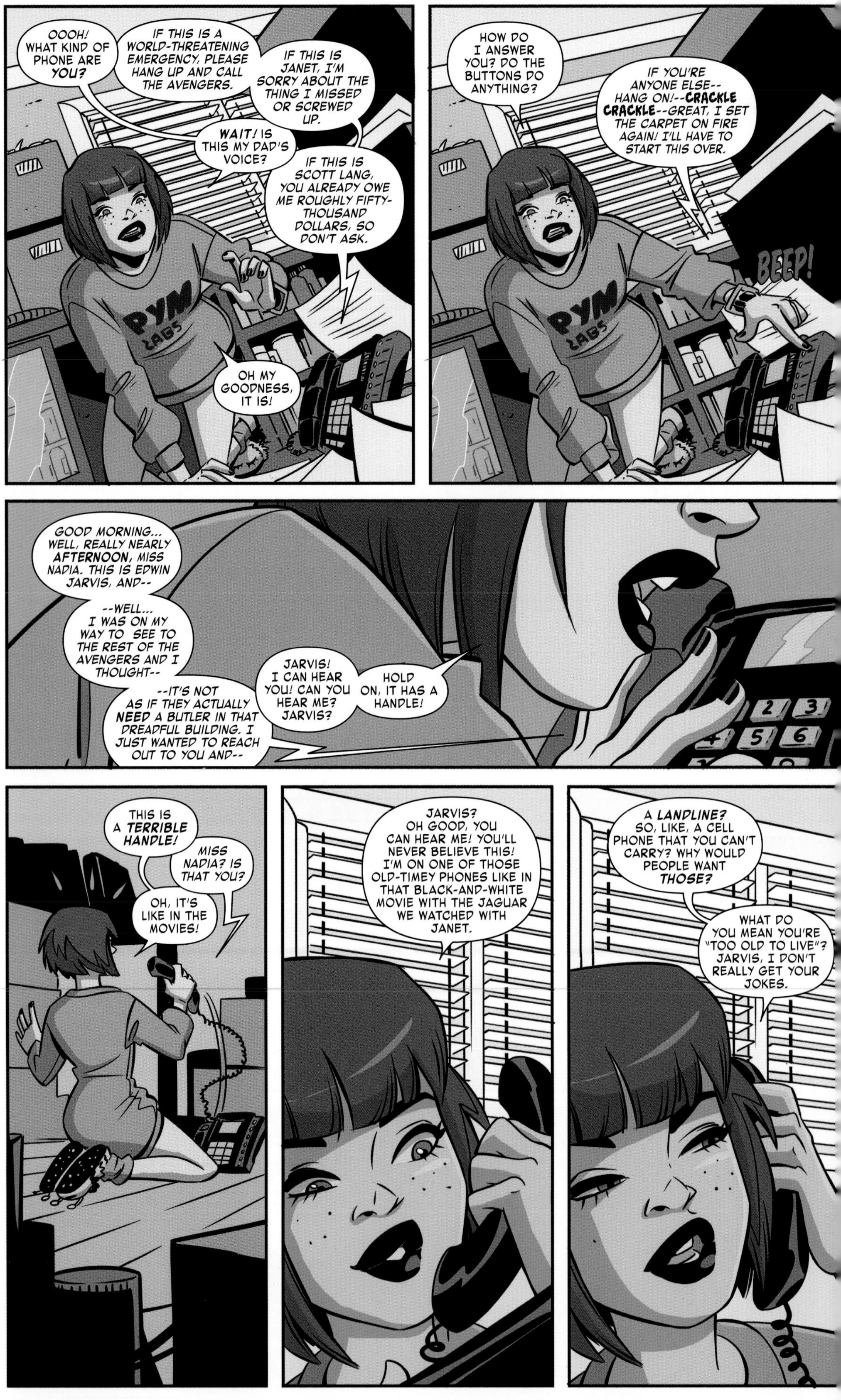
OOOH! WHAT KIND OF PHONE ARE YOU?
IF THIS IS A WORLD-THREATENING EMERGENCY, PLEASE HANG UP AND CALL THE AVENGERS.
IF THIS IS JANET, I'M SORRY ABOUT THE THING I MISSED OR SCREWED UP.
WAIT! IS THIS MY DAD'S VOICE?
IF THIS IS SCOTT LANG, YOU ALREADY OWE ME ROUGHLY FIFTY-THOUSAND DOLLARS, SO DON'T ASK.
OH MY GOODNESS, IT IS!
PYM LABS
HOW DO I ANSWER YOU? DO THE BUTTONS DO ANYTHING?
IF YOU'RE ANYONE ELSE--HANG ON!--CRACKLE CRACKLE--GREAT, I SET THE CARPET ON FIRE AGAIN! I'LL HAVE TO START THIS OVER.
BEEP!
PYM LABS
GOOD MORNING... WELL, REALLY NEARLY AFTERNOON, MISS NADIA. THIS IS EDWIN JARVIS, AND--
--WELL... I WAS ON MY WAY TO SEE TO THE REST OF THE AVENGERS AND I THOUGHT--
--IT'S NOT AS IF THEY ACTUALLY NEED A BUTLER IN THAT DREADFUL BUILDING. I JUST WANTED TO REACH OUT TO YOU AND--
JARVIS! I CAN HEAR YOU! CAN YOU HEAR ME? JARVIS?
HOLD ON, IT HAS A HANDLE!
THIS IS A TERRIBLE HANDLE!
MISS NADIA? IS THAT YOU?
OH, IT'S LIKE IN THE MOVIES!
JARVIS? OH GOOD, YOU CAN HEAR ME! YOU'LL NEVER BELIEVE THIS! I'M ON ONE OF THOSE OLD-TIMEY PHONES LIKE IN THAT BLACK-AND-WHITE MOVIE WITH THE JAGUAR WE WATCHED WITH JANET.
A LANDLINE? SO, LIKE, A CELL PHONE THAT YOU CAN'T CARRY? WHY WOULD PEOPLE WANT THOSE?
WHAT DO YOU MEAN YOU'RE "TOO OLD TO LIVE"? JARVIS, I DON'T REALLY GET YOUR JOKES.

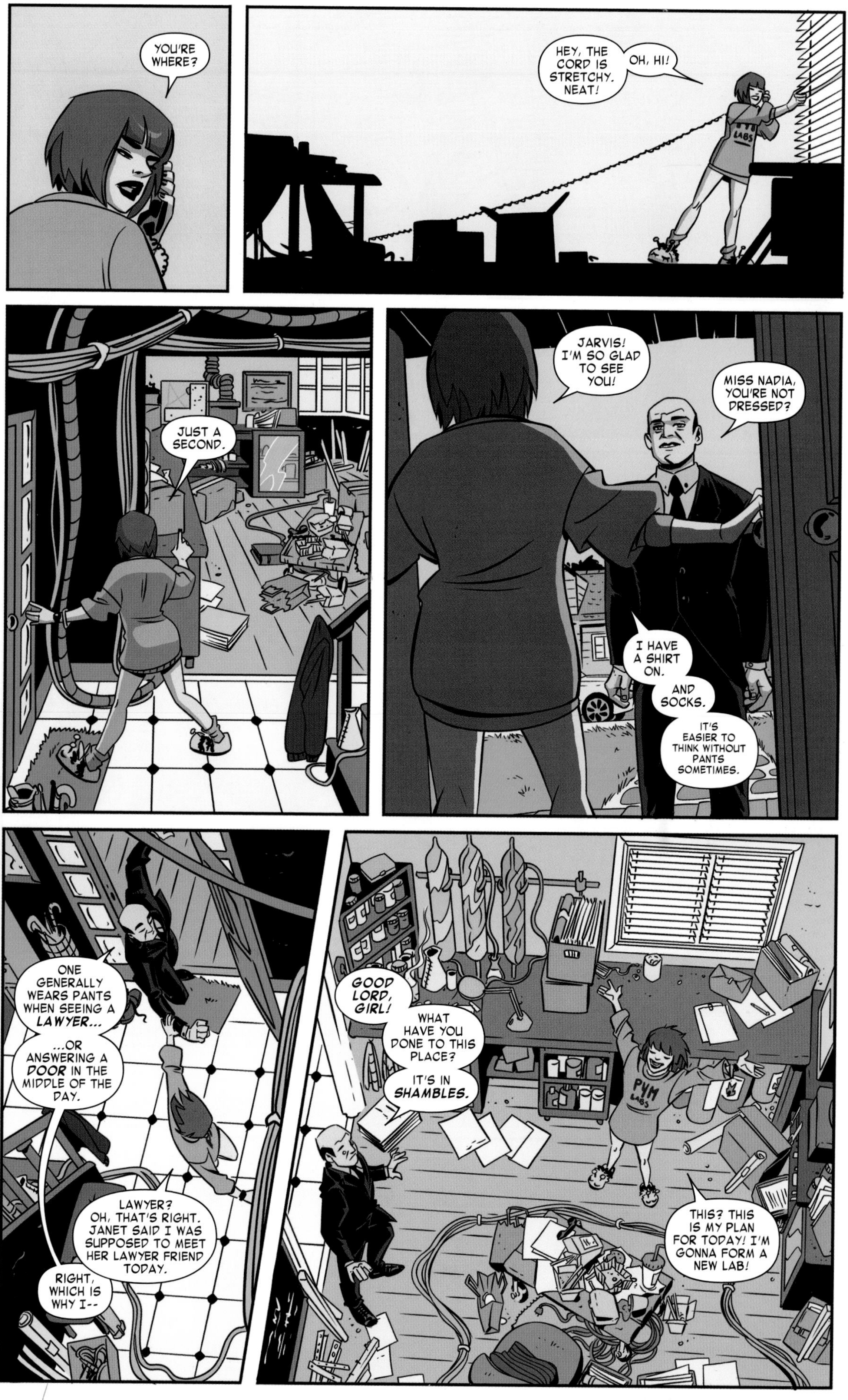

YOU'RE WHERE?
HEY, THE CORD IS STRETCHY. NEAT!
OH, HI!
JUST A SECOND.
JARVIS! I'M SO GLAD TO SEE YOU!
MISS NADIA, YOU'RE NOT DRESSED?
I HAVE A SHIRT ON.
AND SOCKS.
IT'S EASIER TO THINK WITHOUT PANTS SOMETIMES.
ONE GENERALLY WEARS PANTS WHEN SEEING A LAWYER...
...OR ANSWERING A DOOR IN THE MIDDLE OF THE DAY.
LAWYER? OH, THAT'S RIGHT. JANET SAID I WAS SUPPOSED TO MEET HER LAWYER FRIEND TODAY.
RIGHT, WHICH IS WHY I--
GOOD LORD, GIRL!
WHAT HAVE YOU DONE TO THIS PLACE?
IT'S IN SHAMBLES.
THIS? THIS IS MY PLAN FOR TODAY! I'M GONNA FORM A NEW LAB!

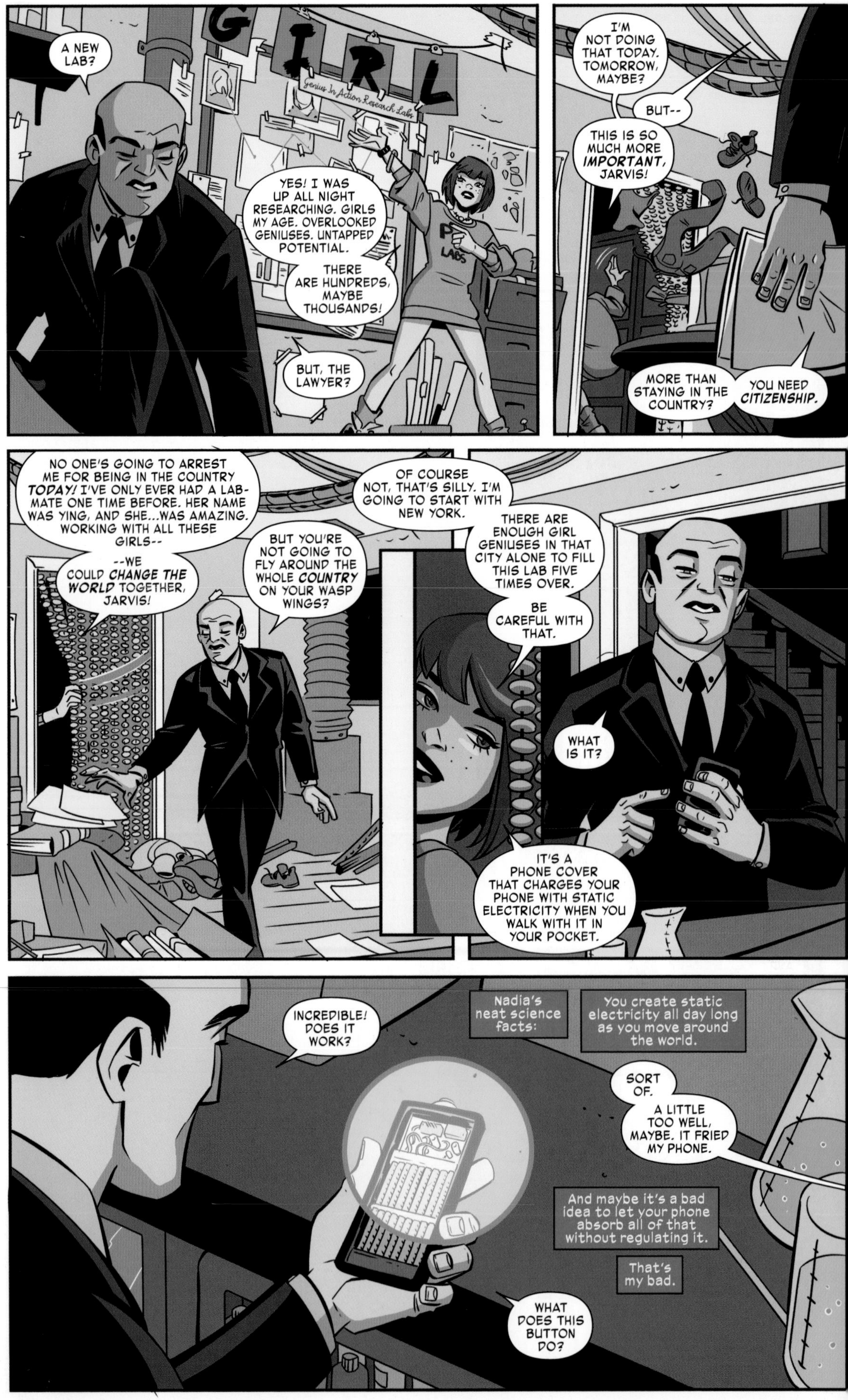
GIRL
Genius In Action Research Labs
A NEW LAB?
YES! I WAS UP ALL NIGHT RESEARCHING. GIRLS MY AGE. OVERLOOKED GENIUSES. UNTAPPED POTENTIAL.
THERE ARE HUNDREDS, MAYBE THOUSANDS!
BUT, THE LAWYER?
I'M NOT DOING THAT TODAY. TOMORROW, MAYBE?
BUT--
THIS IS SO MUCH MORE IMPORTANT, JARVIS!
MORE THAN STAYING IN THE COUNTRY?
YOU NEED CITIZENSHIP.
NO ONE'S GOING TO ARREST ME FOR BEING IN THE COUNTRY TODAY! I'VE ONLY EVER HAD A LAB-MATE ONE TIME BEFORE. HER NAME WAS YING, AND SHE...WAS AMAZING. WORKING WITH ALL THESE GIRLS--
--WE COULD CHANGE THE WORLD TOGETHER, JARVIS!
BUT YOU'RE NOT GOING TO FLY AROUND THE WHOLE COUNTRY ON YOUR WASP WINGS?
OF COURSE NOT, THAT'S SILLY. I'M GOING TO START WITH NEW YORK.
THERE ARE ENOUGH GIRL GENIUSES IN THAT CITY ALONE TO FILL THIS LAB FIVE TIMES OVER.
BE CAREFUL WITH THAT.
WHAT IS IT?
IT'S A PHONE COVER THAT CHARGES YOUR PHONE WITH STATIC ELECTRICITY WHEN YOU WALK WITH IT IN YOUR POCKET.
INCREDIBLE! DOES IT WORK?
Nadia's neat science facts:
You create static electricity all day long as you move around the world.
SORT OF.
A LITTLE TOO WELL, MAYBE. IT FRIED MY PHONE.
And maybe it's a bad idea to let your phone absorb all of that without regulating it.
That's my bad.
WHAT DOES THIS BUTTON DO?

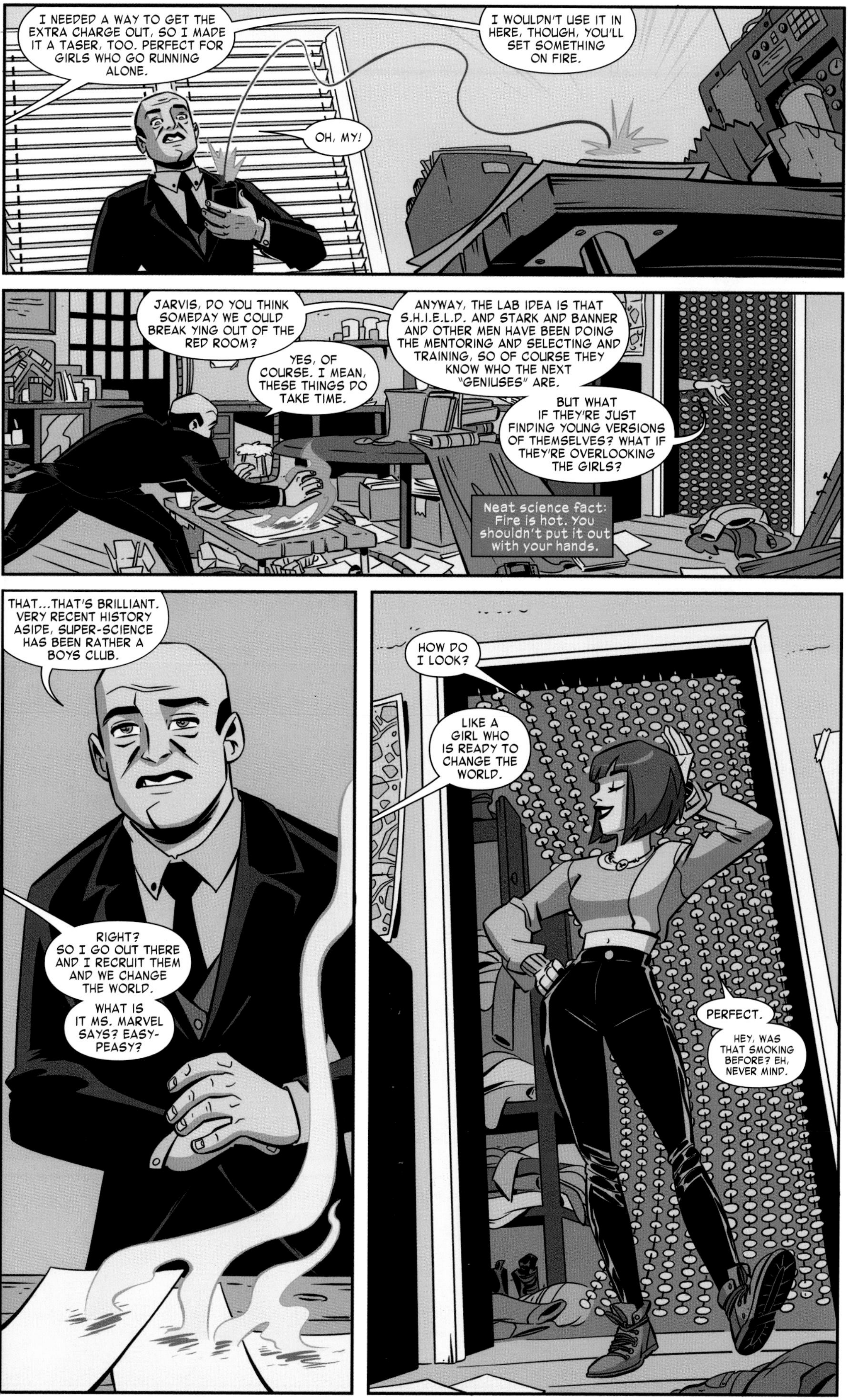
I NEEDED A WAY TO GET THE EXTRA CHARGE OUT, SO I MADE IT A TASER, TOO. PERFECT FOR GIRLS WHO GO RUNNING ALONE.
I WOULDN'T USE IT IN HERE, THOUGH, YOU'LL SET SOMETHING ON FIRE.
OH, MY!
JARVIS, DO YOU THINK SOMEDAY WE COULD BREAK YING OUT OF THE RED ROOM?
YES, OF COURSE. I MEAN, THESE THINGS DO TAKE TIME.
ANYWAY, THE LAB IDEA IS THAT S.H.I.E.L.D. AND STARK AND BANNER AND OTHER MEN HAVE BEEN DOING THE MENTORING AND SELECTING AND TRAINING, SO OF COURSE THEY KNOW WHO THE NEXT "GENIUSES" ARE.
BUT WHAT IF THEY'RE JUST FINDING YOUNG VERSIONS OF THEMSELVES? WHAT IF THEY'RE OVERLOOKING THE GIRLS?
Neat science fact: Fire is hot. You shouldn't put it out with your hands.
THAT...THAT'S BRILLIANT. VERY RECENT HISTORY ASIDE, SUPER-SCIENCE HAS BEEN RATHER A BOYS CLUB.
RIGHT? SO I GO OUT THERE AND I RECRUIT THEM AND WE CHANGE THE WORLD.
WHAT IS IT MS. MARVEL SAYS? EASY-PEASY?
HOW DO I LOOK?
LIKE A GIRL WHO IS READY TO CHANGE THE WORLD.
PERFECT.
HEY, WAS THAT SMOKING BEFORE? EH, NEVER MIND.

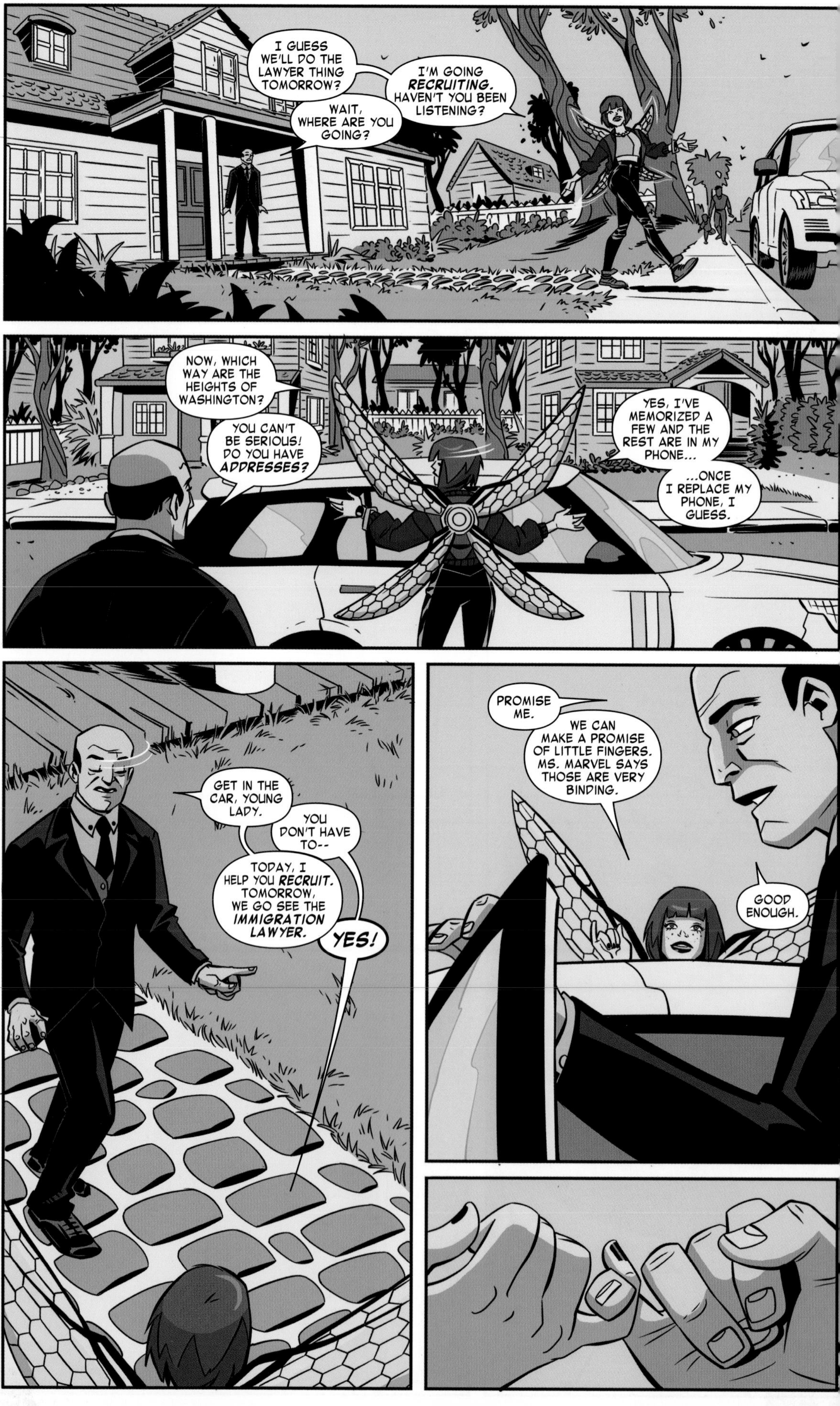
I GUESS WE'LL DO THE LAWYER THING TOMORROW?
I'M GOING RECRUITING. HAVEN'T YOU BEEN LISTENING?
WAIT, WHERE ARE YOU GOING?
NOW, WHICH WAY ARE THE HEIGHTS OF WASHINGTON?
YOU CAN'T BE SERIOUS! DO YOU HAVE ADDRESSES?
YES, I'VE MEMORIZED A FEW AND THE REST ARE IN MY PHONE...
...ONCE I REPLACE MY PHONE, I GUESS.
GET IN THE CAR, YOUNG LADY.
YOU DON'T HAVE TO--
TODAY, I HELP YOU RECRUIT. TOMORROW, WE GO SEE THE IMMIGRATION LAWYER.
YES!
PROMISE ME.
WE CAN MAKE A PROMISE OF LITTLE FINGERS. MS. MARVEL SAYS THOSE ARE VERY BINDING.
GOOD ENOUGH.

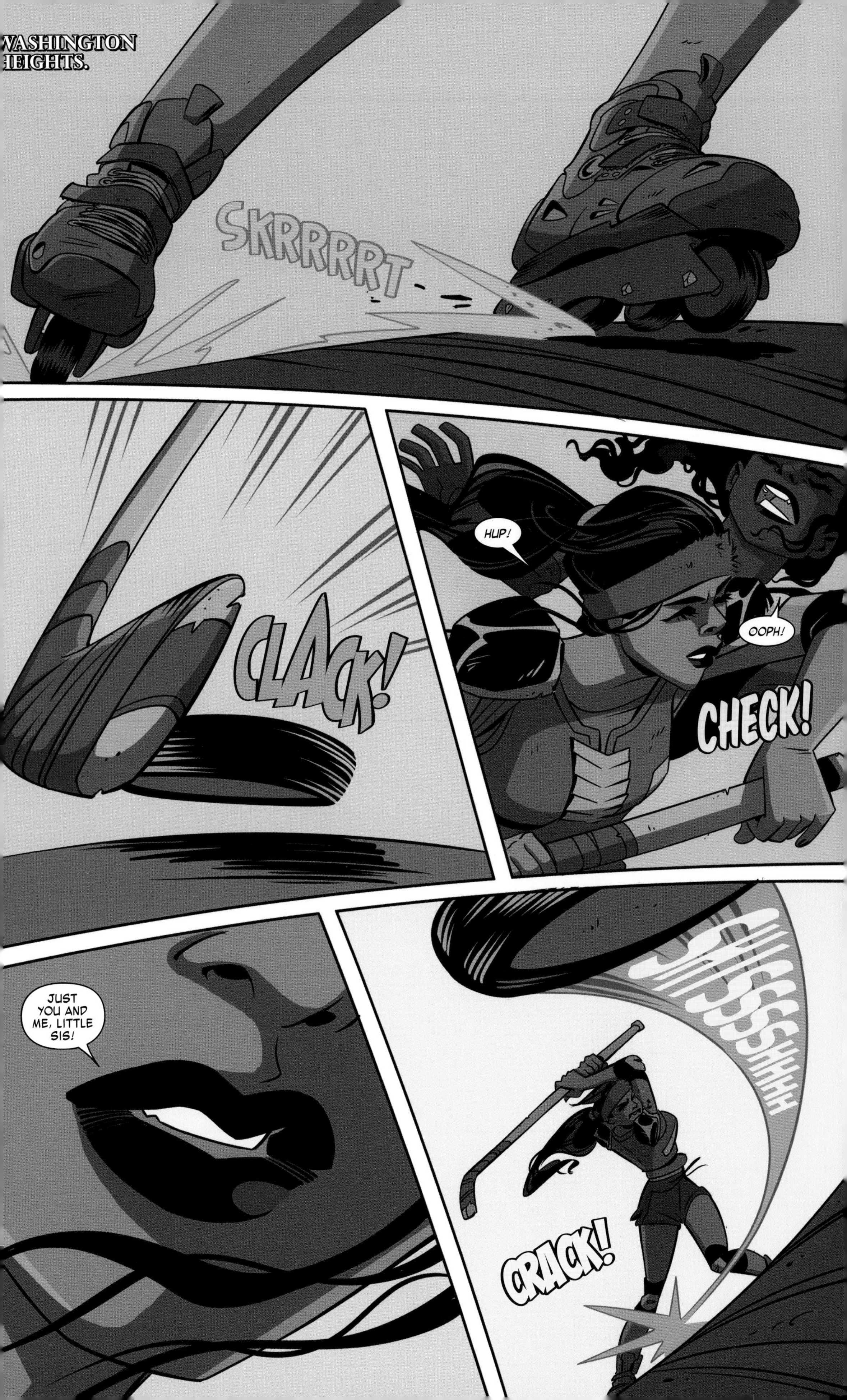
WASHINGTON HEIGHTS.
SKRRRRT
CLACK!
HUP!
OOPH!
CHECK!
JUST YOU AND ME, LITTLE SIS!
SHHSSSSHHHH
CRACK!

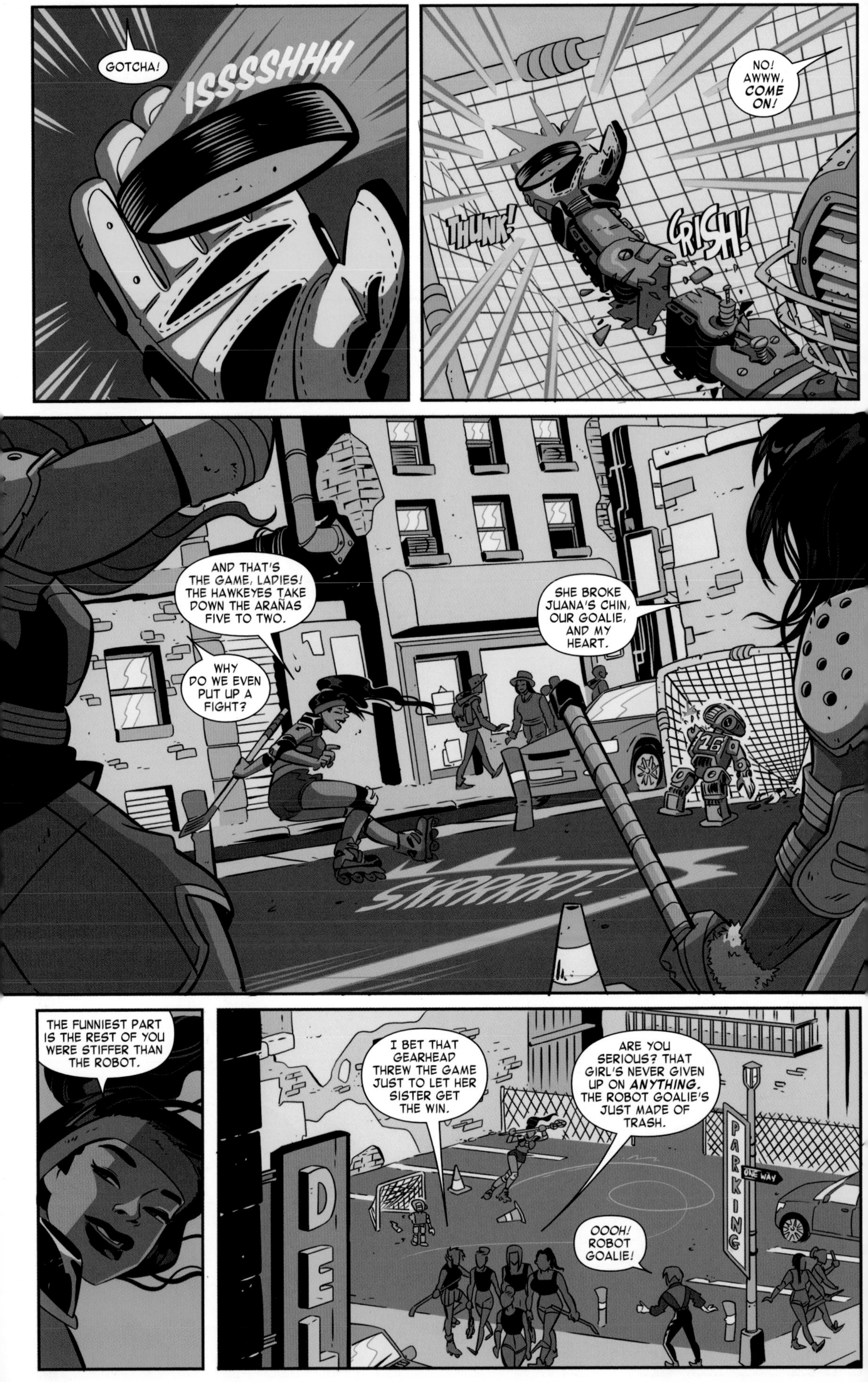
GOTCHA!
ISSSSHHH
NO! AWWW, COME ON!
THUNK!
CRISH!
AND THAT'S THE GAME, LADIES! THE HAWKEYES TAKE DOWN THE ARAÑAS FIVE TO TWO.
WHY DO WE EVEN PUT UP A FIGHT?
SHE BROKE JUANA'S CHIN, OUR GOALIE, AND MY HEART.
SKRRRRT!
THE FUNNIEST PART IS THE REST OF YOU WERE STIFFER THAN THE ROBOT.
I BET THAT GEARHEAD THREW THE GAME JUST TO LET HER SISTER GET THE WIN.
ARE YOU SERIOUS? THAT GIRL'S NEVER GIVEN UP ON ANYTHING. THE ROBOT GOALIE'S JUST MADE OF TRASH.
OOOH! ROBOT GOALIE!
DELI
PARKING
ONE WAY

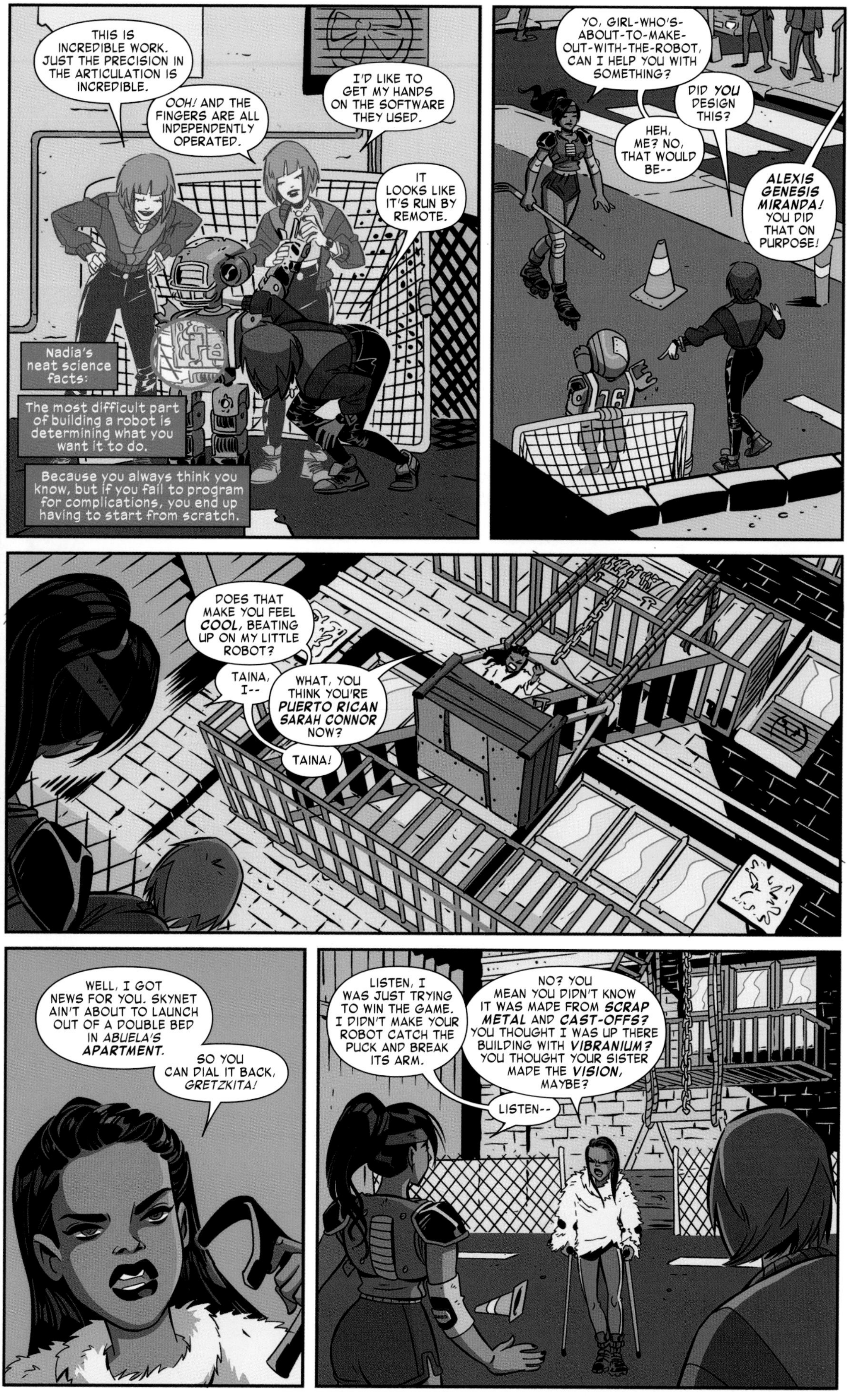
THIS IS INCREDIBLE WORK. JUST THE PRECISION IN THE ARTICULATION IS INCREDIBLE.
OOH! AND THE FINGERS ARE ALL INDEPENDENTLY OPERATED.
I'D LIKE TO GET MY HANDS ON THE SOFTWARE THEY USED.
IT LOOKS LIKE IT'S RUN BY REMOTE.
Nadia's neat science facts:
The most difficult part of building a robot is determining what you want it to do.
Because you always think you know, but if you fail to program for complications, you end up having to start from scratch.
YO, GIRL-WHO'S-ABOUT-TO-MAKE-OUT-WITH-THE-ROBOT, CAN I HELP YOU WITH SOMETHING?
DID YOU DESIGN THIS?
HEH, ME? NO, THAT WOULD BE--
ALEXIS GENESIS MIRANDA! YOU DID THAT ON PURPOSE!
16
DOES THAT MAKE YOU FEEL COOL, BEATING UP ON MY LITTLE ROBOT?
TAINA, I--
WHAT, YOU THINK YOU'RE PUERTO RICAN SARAH CONNOR NOW?
TAINA!
WELL, I GOT NEWS FOR YOU. SKYNET AIN'T ABOUT TO LAUNCH OUT OF A DOUBLE BED IN ABUELA'S APARTMENT.
SO YOU CAN DIAL IT BACK, GRETZKITA!
LISTEN, I WAS JUST TRYING TO WIN THE GAME. I DIDN'T MAKE YOUR ROBOT CATCH THE PUCK AND BREAK ITS ARM.
NO? YOU MEAN YOU DIDN'T KNOW IT WAS MADE FROM SCRAP METAL AND CAST-OFFS? YOU THOUGHT I WAS UP THERE BUILDING WITH VIBRANIUM? YOU THOUGHT YOUR SISTER MADE THE VISION, MAYBE?
LISTEN--

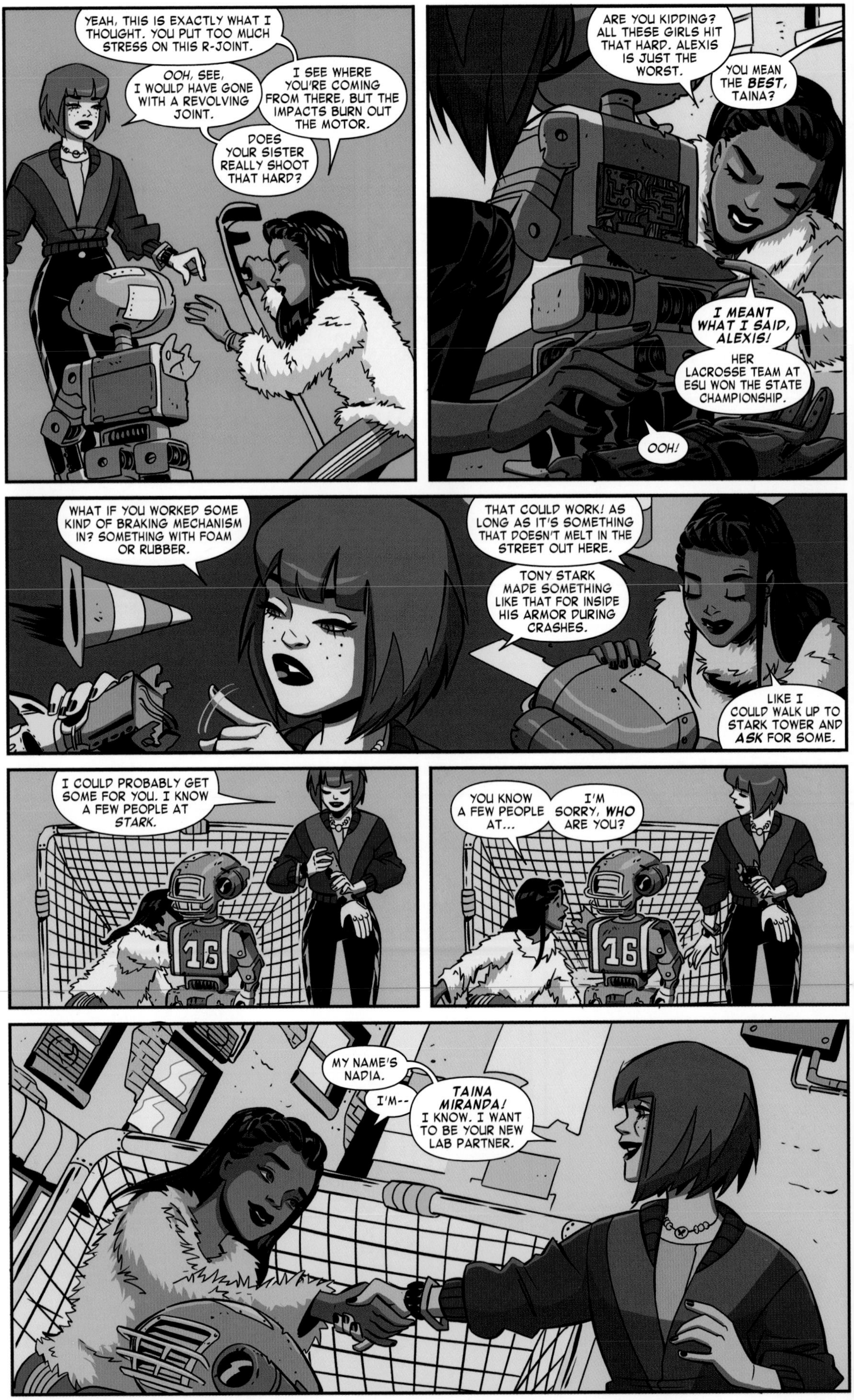
YEAH, THIS IS EXACTLY WHAT I THOUGHT. YOU PUT TOO MUCH STRESS ON THIS R-JOINT.
OOH, SEE, I WOULD HAVE GONE WITH A REVOLVING JOINT.
I SEE WHERE YOU'RE COMING FROM THERE, BUT THE IMPACTS BURN OUT THE MOTOR.
DOES YOUR SISTER REALLY SHOOT THAT HARD?
ARE YOU KIDDING? ALL THESE GIRLS HIT THAT HARD. ALEXIS IS JUST THE WORST.
YOU MEAN THE BEST, TAINA?
I MEANT WHAT I SAID, ALEXIS!
HER LACROSSE TEAM AT ESU WON THE STATE CHAMPIONSHIP.
OOH!
WHAT IF YOU WORKED SOME KIND OF BRAKING MECHANISM IN? SOMETHING WITH FOAM OR RUBBER.
THAT COULD WORK! AS LONG AS IT'S SOMETHING THAT DOESN'T MELT IN THE STREET OUT HERE.
TONY STARK MADE SOMETHING LIKE THAT FOR INSIDE HIS ARMOR DURING CRASHES.
LIKE I COULD WALK UP TO STARK TOWER AND ASK FOR SOME.
I COULD PROBABLY GET SOME FOR YOU. I KNOW A FEW PEOPLE AT STARK.
YOU KNOW A FEW PEOPLE AT...
I'M SORRY, WHO ARE YOU?
MY NAME'S NADIA.
I'M--
TAINA MIRANDA! I KNOW. I WANT TO BE YOUR NEW LAB PARTNER.

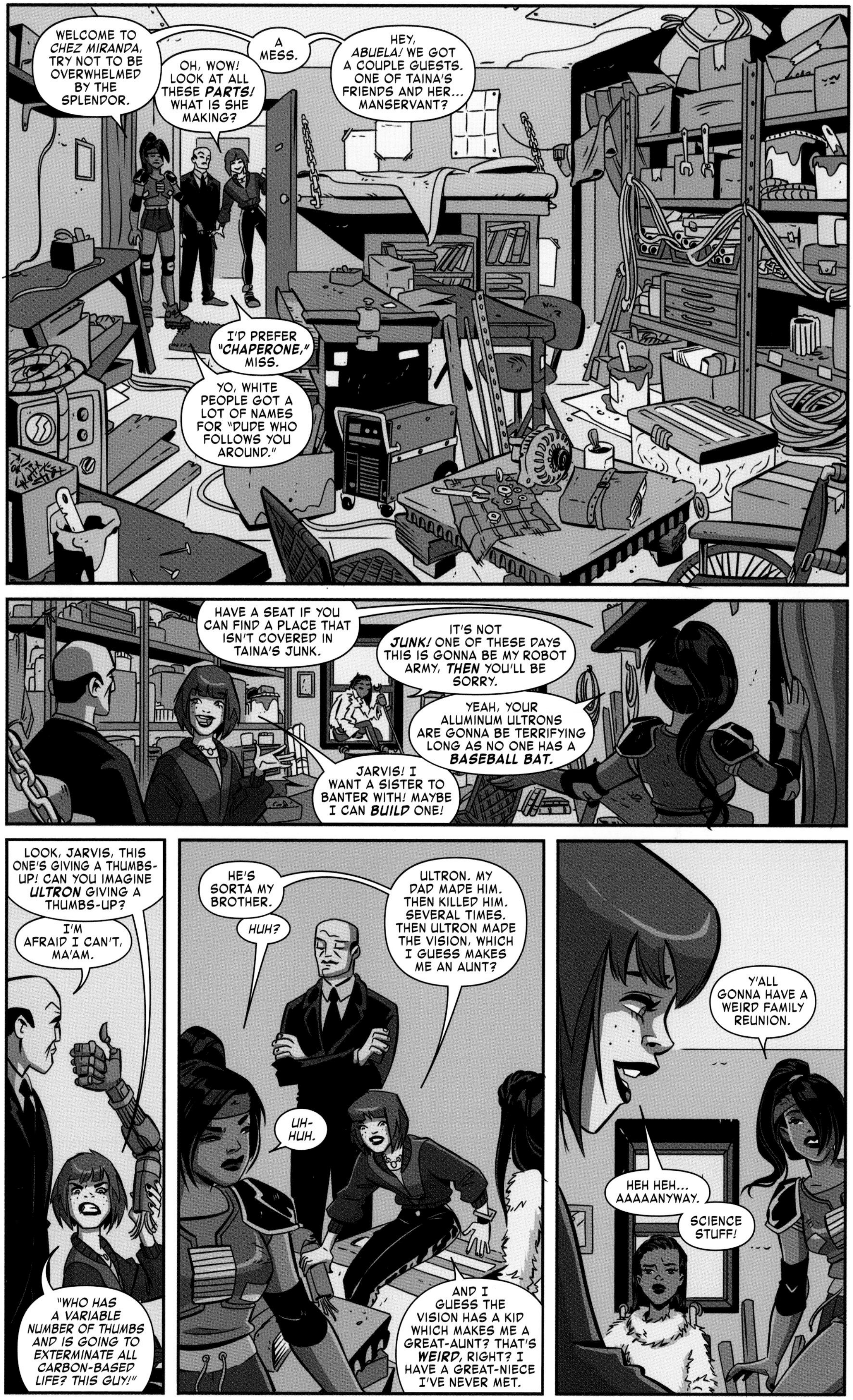
WELCOME TO CHEZ MIRANDA. TRY NOT TO BE OVERWHELMED BY THE SPLENDOR.
A MESS.
OH, WOW! LOOK AT ALL THESE PARTS! WHAT IS SHE MAKING?
HEY, ABUELA! WE GOT A COUPLE GUESTS. ONE OF TAINA'S FRIENDS AND HER... MANSERVANT?
I'D PREFER "CHAPERONE," MISS.
YO, WHITE PEOPLE GOT A LOT OF NAMES FOR "DUDE WHO FOLLOWS YOU AROUND."
HAVE A SEAT IF YOU CAN FIND A PLACE THAT ISN'T COVERED IN TAINA'S JUNK.
IT'S NOT JUNK! ONE OF THESE DAYS THIS IS GONNA BE MY ROBOT ARMY, THEN YOU'LL BE SORRY.
YEAH, YOUR ALUMINUM ULTRONS ARE GONNA BE TERRIFYING LONG AS NO ONE HAS A BASEBALL BAT.
JARVIS! I WANT A SISTER TO BANTER WITH! MAYBE I CAN BUILD ONE!
LOOK, JARVIS, THIS ONE'S GIVING A THUMBS-UP! CAN YOU IMAGINE ULTRON GIVING A THUMBS-UP?
I'M AFRAID I CAN'T, MA'AM.
"WHO HAS A VARIABLE NUMBER OF THUMBS AND IS GOING TO EXTERMINATE ALL CARBON-BASED LIFE? THIS GUY!"
HE'S SORTA MY BROTHER.
HUH?
ULTRON. MY DAD MADE HIM. THEN KILLED HIM. SEVERAL TIMES. THEN ULTRON MADE THE VISION, WHICH I GUESS MAKES ME AN AUNT?
UH-HUH.
AND I GUESS THE VISION HAS A KID WHICH MAKES ME A GREAT-AUNT? THAT'S WEIRD, RIGHT? I HAVE A GREAT-NIECE I'VE NEVER MET.
Y'ALL GONNA HAVE A WEIRD FAMILY REUNION.
HEH HEH... AAAAANYWAY.
SCIENCE STUFF!

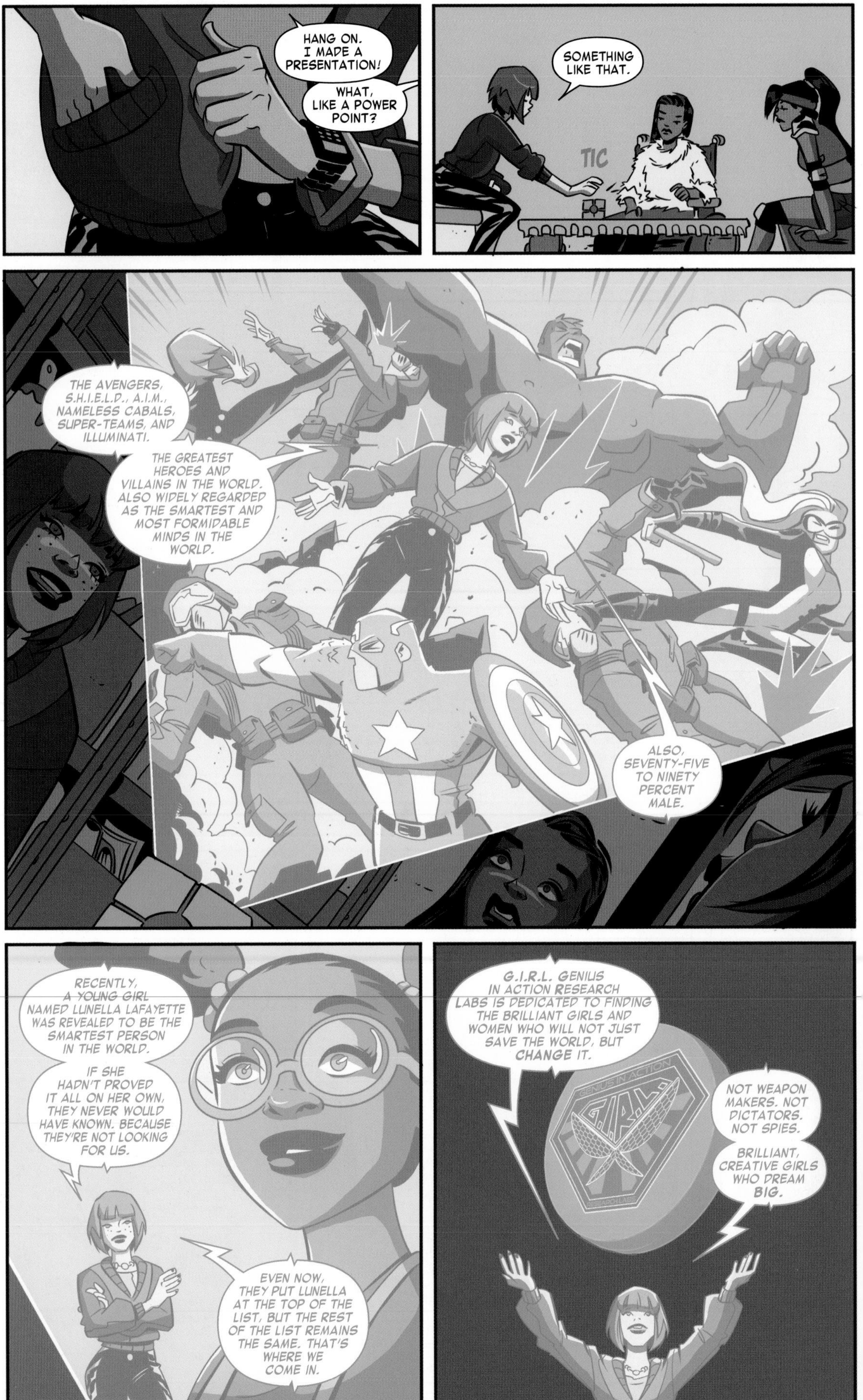
HANG ON. I MADE A PRESENTATION!
WHAT, LIKE A POWER POINT?
SOMETHING LIKE THAT.
TIC
THE AVENGERS, S.H.I.E.L.D., A.I.M., NAMELESS CABALS, SUPER-TEAMS, AND ILLUMINATI.
THE GREATEST HEROES AND VILLAINS IN THE WORLD. ALSO WIDELY REGARDED AS THE SMARTEST AND MOST FORMIDABLE MINDS IN THE WORLD.
ALSO, SEVENTY-FIVE TO NINETY PERCENT MALE.
RECENTLY, A YOUNG GIRL NAMED LUNELLA LAFAYETTE WAS REVEALED TO BE THE SMARTEST PERSON IN THE WORLD.
IF SHE HADN'T PROVED IT ALL ON HER OWN, THEY NEVER WOULD HAVE KNOWN. BECAUSE THEY'RE NOT LOOKING FOR US.
EVEN NOW, THEY PUT LUNELLA AT THE TOP OF THE LIST, BUT THE REST OF THE LIST REMAINS THE SAME. THAT'S WHERE WE COME IN.
G.I.R.L. GENIUS IN ACTION RESEARCH LABS IS DEDICATED TO FINDING THE BRILLIANT GIRLS AND WOMEN WHO WILL NOT JUST SAVE THE WORLD, BUT CHANGE IT.
GENIUS IN ACTION
NOT WEAPON MAKERS. NOT DICTATORS. NOT SPIES.
BRILLIANT, CREATIVE GIRLS WHO DREAM BIG.

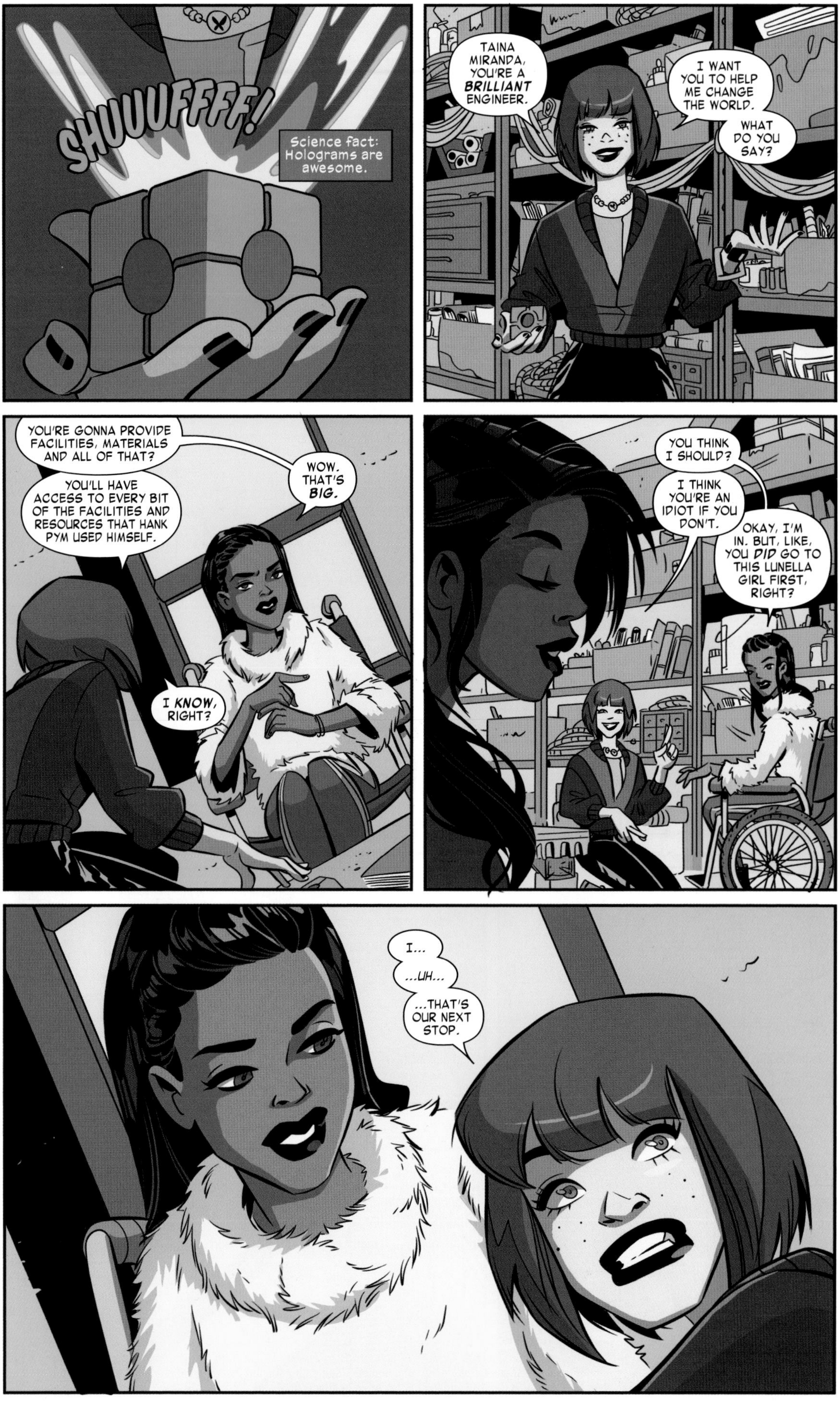

SHUUUFFFF!
Science fact: Holograms are awesome.
TAINA MIRANDA, YOU'RE A BRILLIANT ENGINEER.
I WANT YOU TO HELP ME CHANGE THE WORLD.
WHAT DO YOU SAY?
YOU'RE GONNA PROVIDE FACILITIES, MATERIALS AND ALL OF THAT?
YOU'LL HAVE ACCESS TO EVERY BIT OF THE FACILITIES AND RESOURCES THAT HANK PYM USED HIMSELF.
WOW. THAT'S BIG.
I KNOW, RIGHT?
YOU THINK I SHOULD?
I THINK YOU'RE AN IDIOT IF YOU DON'T.
OKAY, I'M IN. BUT, LIKE, YOU DID GO TO THIS LUNELLA GIRL FIRST, RIGHT?
I...
...UH...
...THAT'S OUR NEXT STOP.

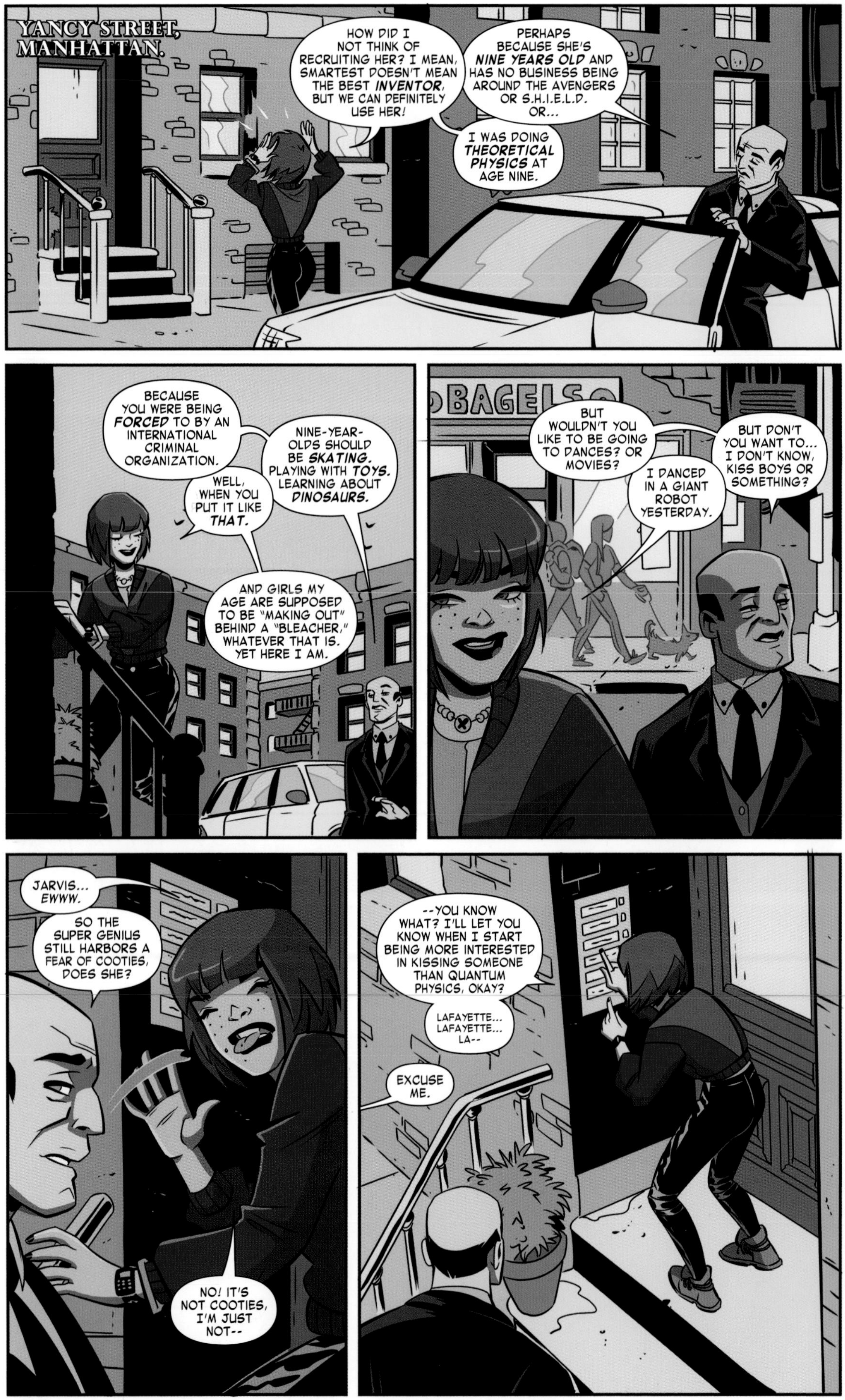
YANCY STREET, MANHATTAN.
HOW DID I NOT THINK OF RECRUITING HER? I MEAN, SMARTEST DOESN'T MEAN THE BEST INVENTOR, BUT WE CAN DEFINITELY USE HER!
PERHAPS BECAUSE SHE'S NINE YEARS OLD AND HAS NO BUSINESS BEING AROUND THE AVENGERS OR S.H.I.E.L.D. OR...
I WAS DOING THEORETICAL PHYSICS AT AGE NINE.
BECAUSE YOU WERE BEING FORCED TO BY AN INTERNATIONAL CRIMINAL ORGANIZATION.
WELL, WHEN YOU PUT IT LIKE THAT.
NINE-YEAR-OLDS SHOULD BE SKATING. PLAYING WITH TOYS. LEARNING ABOUT DINOSAURS.
AND GIRLS MY AGE ARE SUPPOSED TO BE "MAKING OUT" BEHIND A "BLEACHER," WHATEVER THAT IS. YET HERE I AM.
BAGELS
BUT WOULDN'T YOU LIKE TO BE GOING TO DANCES? OR MOVIES?
I DANCED IN A GIANT ROBOT YESTERDAY.
BUT DON'T YOU WANT TO... I DON'T KNOW, KISS BOYS OR SOMETHING?
JARVIS... EWWW.
SO THE SUPER GENIUS STILL HARBORS A FEAR OF COOTIES, DOES SHE?
NO! IT'S NOT COOTIES, I'M JUST NOT--
--YOU KNOW WHAT? I'LL LET YOU KNOW WHEN I START BEING MORE INTERESTED IN KISSING SOMEONE THAN QUANTUM PHYSICS, OKAY?
LAFAYETTE... LAFAYETTE... LA--
EXCUSE ME.

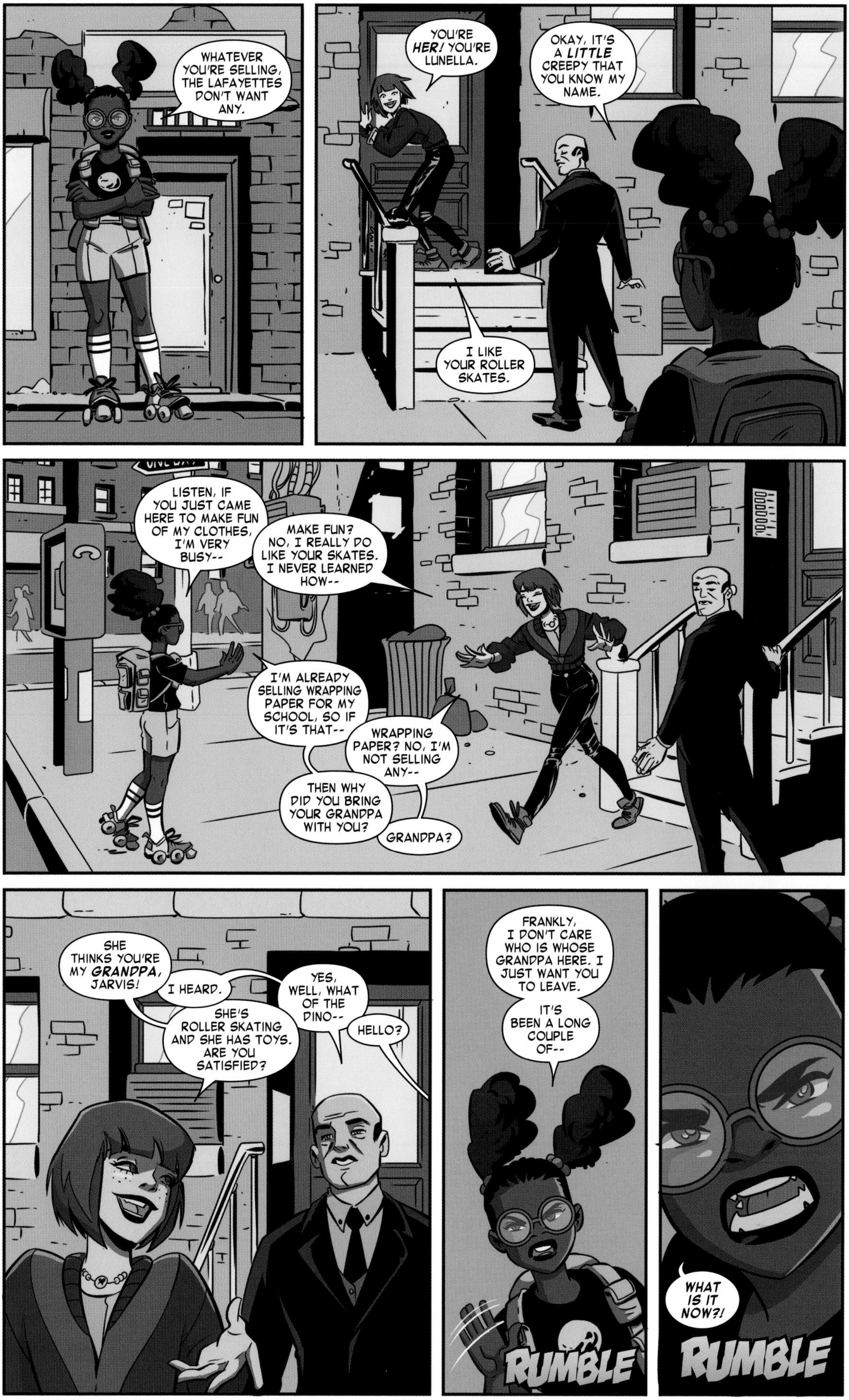
WHATEVER YOU'RE SELLING, THE LAFAYETTES DON'T WANT ANY.
YOU'RE HER! YOU'RE LUNELLA.
OKAY, IT'S A LITTLE CREEPY THAT YOU KNOW MY NAME.
I LIKE YOUR ROLLER SKATES.
ONE WAY
LISTEN, IF YOU JUST CAME HERE TO MAKE FUN OF MY CLOTHES, I'M VERY BUSY--
MAKE FUN? NO, I REALLY DO LIKE YOUR SKATES. I NEVER LEARNED HOW--
I'M ALREADY SELLING WRAPPING PAPER FOR MY SCHOOL, SO IF IT'S THAT--
WRAPPING PAPER? NO, I'M NOT SELLING ANY--
THEN WHY DID YOU BRING YOUR GRANDPA WITH YOU?
GRANDPA?
SHE THINKS YOU'RE MY GRANDPA, JARVIS!
I HEARD.
SHE'S ROLLER SKATING AND SHE HAS TOYS. ARE YOU SATISFIED?
YES, WELL, WHAT OF THE DINO--
HELLO?
FRANKLY, I DON'T CARE WHO IS WHOSE GRANDPA HERE. I JUST WANT YOU TO LEAVE.
IT'S BEEN A LONG COUPLE OF--
RUMBLE
WHAT IS IT NOW?!
RUMBLE

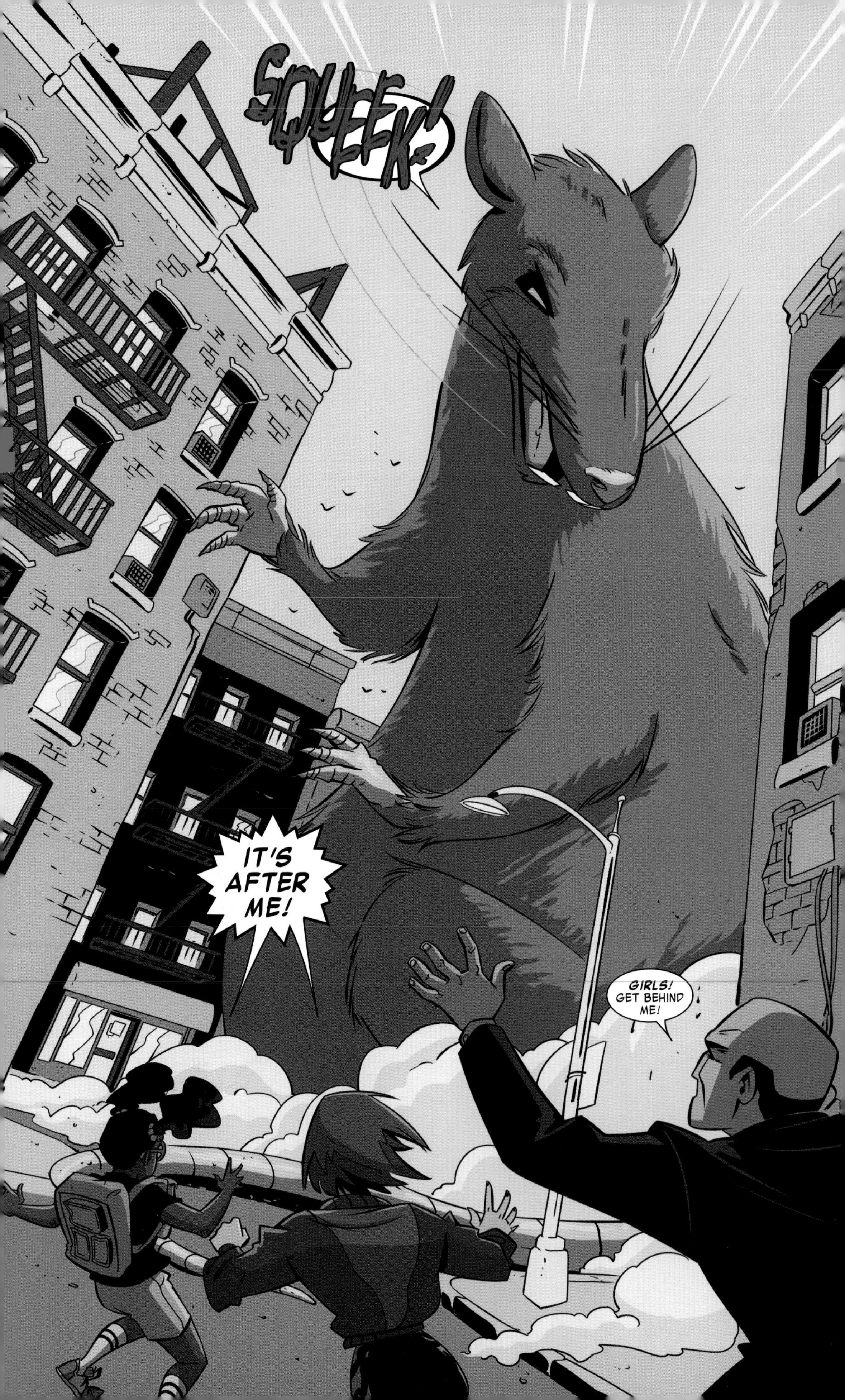
SQUEEK!
IT'S AFTER ME!
GIRLS! GET BEHIND ME!

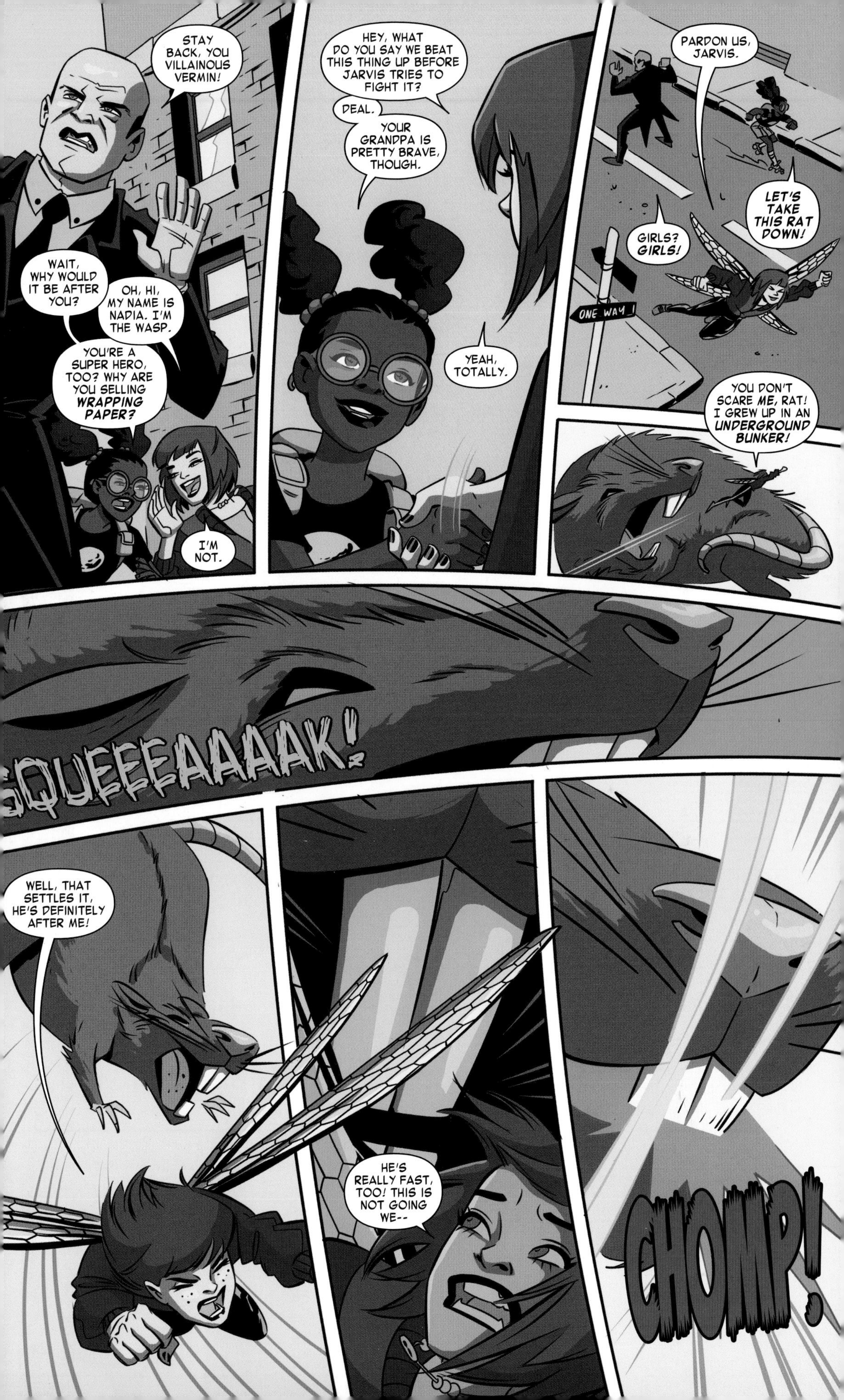
STAY BACK, YOU VILLAINOUS VERMIN!
WAIT, WHY WOULD IT BE AFTER YOU?
OH, HI, MY NAME IS NADIA. I'M THE WASP.
YOU'RE A SUPER HERO, TOO? WHY ARE YOU SELLING WRAPPING PAPER?
I'M NOT.
HEY, WHAT DO YOU SAY WE BEAT THIS THING UP BEFORE JARVIS TRIES TO FIGHT IT?
DEAL.
YOUR GRANDPA IS PRETTY BRAVE, THOUGH.
YEAH, TOTALLY.
PARDON US, JARVIS.
GIRLS? GIRLS!
LET'S TAKE THIS RAT DOWN!
ONE WAY
YOU DON'T SCARE ME, RAT! I GREW UP IN AN UNDERGROUND BUNKER!
SQUEEEAAAAK!
WELL, THAT SETTLES IT, HE'S DEFINITELY AFTER ME!
HE'S REALLY FAST, TOO! THIS IS NOT GOING WE--
CHOMP!

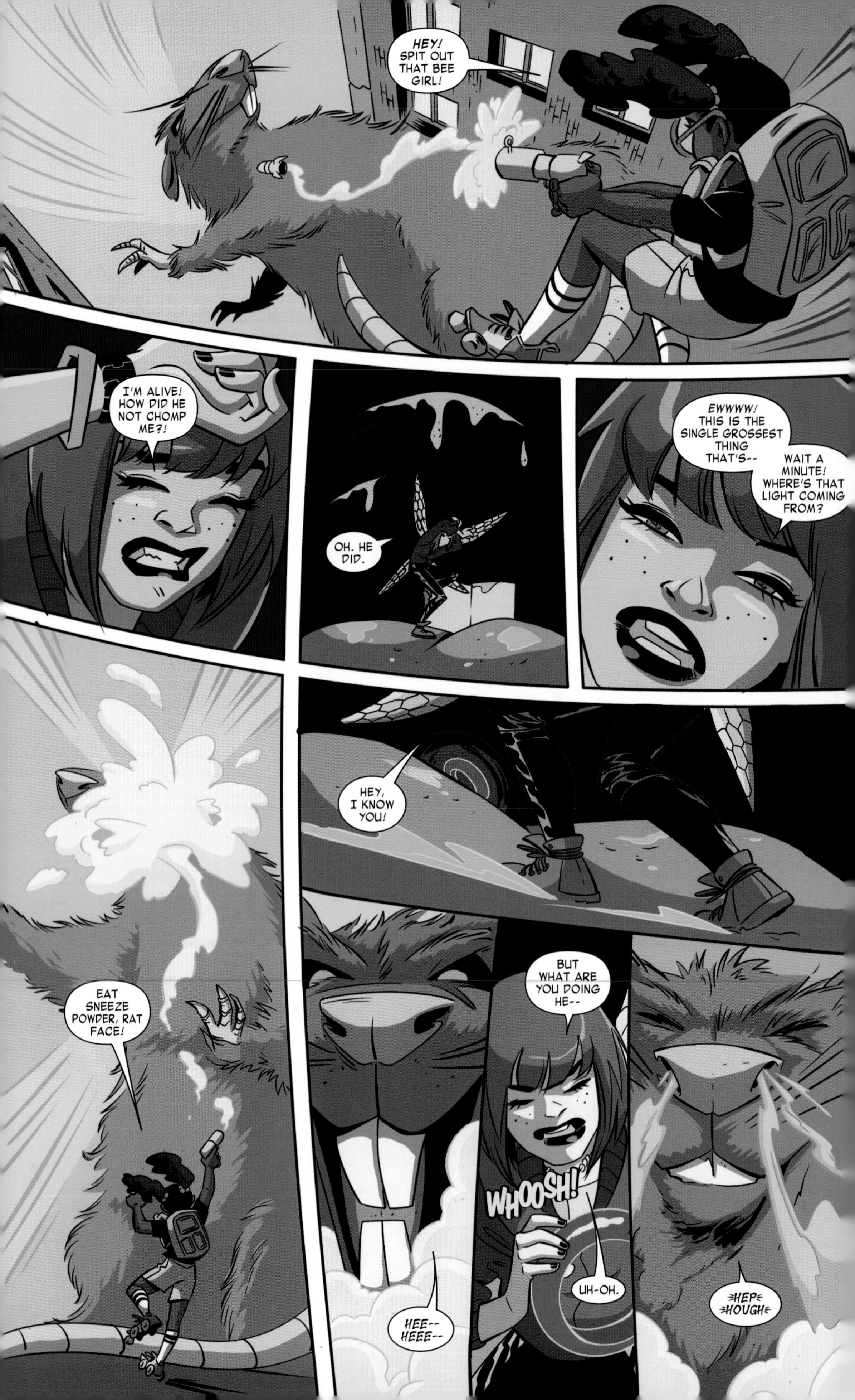
HEY! SPIT OUT THAT BEE GIRL!
I'M ALIVE! HOW DID HE NOT CHOMP ME?!
OH. HE DID.
EWWWW! THIS IS THE SINGLE GROSSEST THING THAT'S--
WAIT A MINUTE! WHERE'S THAT LIGHT COMING FROM?
EAT SNEEZE POWDER, RAT FACE!
HEY, I KNOW YOU!
BUT WHAT ARE YOU DOING HE--
HEE-- HEEE--
WHOOSH!
UH-OH.
HEP HOUGH

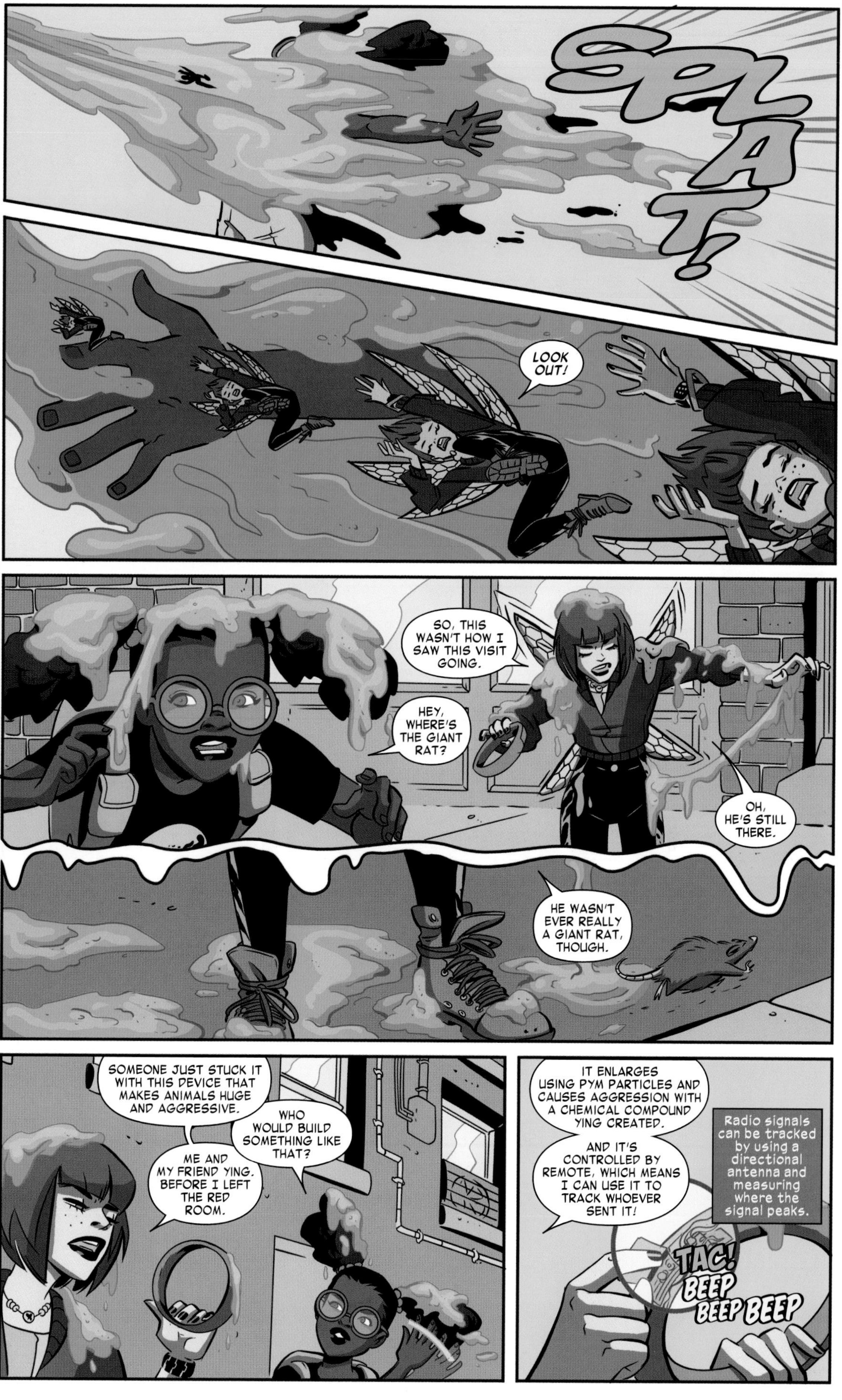
SPLAT!
LOOK OUT!
SO, THIS WASN'T HOW I SAW THIS VISIT GOING.
HEY, WHERE'S THE GIANT RAT?
OH, HE'S STILL THERE.
HE WASN'T EVER REALLY A GIANT RAT, THOUGH.
SOMEONE JUST STUCK IT WITH THIS DEVICE THAT MAKES ANIMALS HUGE AND AGGRESSIVE.
WHO WOULD BUILD SOMETHING LIKE THAT?
ME AND MY FRIEND YING. BEFORE I LEFT THE RED ROOM.
IT ENLARGES USING PYM PARTICLES AND CAUSES AGGRESSION WITH A CHEMICAL COMPOUND YING CREATED.
AND IT'S CONTROLLED BY REMOTE, WHICH MEANS I CAN USE IT TO TRACK WHOEVER SENT IT!
Radio signals can be tracked by using a directional antenna and measuring where the signal peaks.
TAC! BEEP BEEP BEEP BEEP

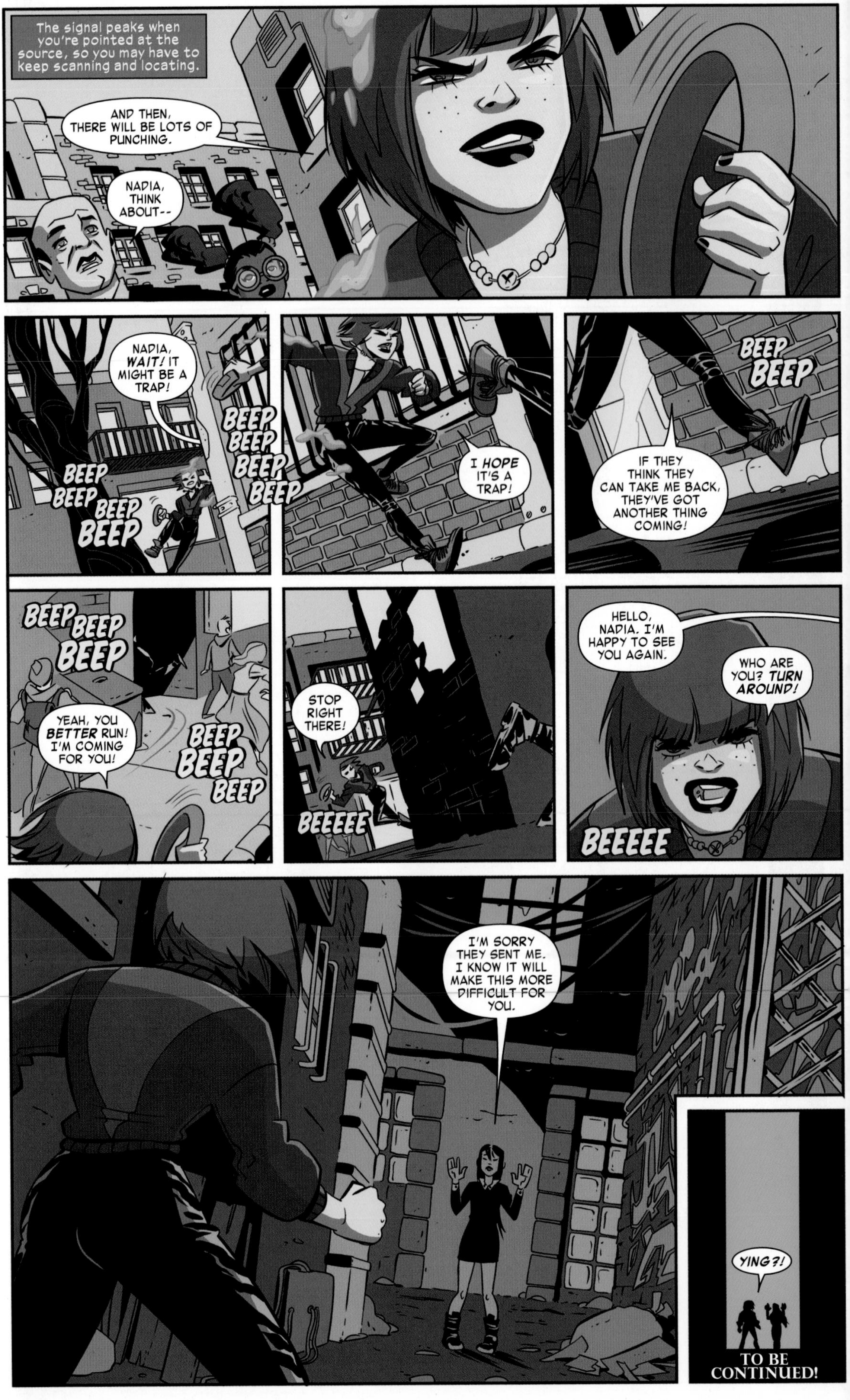

The signal peaks when you're pointed at the source, so you may have to keep scanning and locating.
AND THEN, THERE WILL BE LOTS OF PUNCHING.
NADIA, THINK ABOUT--
NADIA, WAIT! IT MIGHT BE A TRAP!
BEEP BEEP BEEP BEEP
BEEP BEEP BEEP BEEP
I HOPE IT'S A TRAP!
BEEP BEEP
IF THEY THINK THEY CAN TAKE ME BACK, THEY'VE GOT ANOTHER THING COMING!
BEEP BEEP BEEP
YEAH, YOU BETTER RUN! I'M COMING FOR YOU!
BEEP BEEP BEEP
STOP RIGHT THERE!
BEEEEE
HELLO, NADIA. I'M HAPPY TO SEE YOU AGAIN.
WHO ARE YOU? TURN AROUND!
BEEEEE
I'M SORRY THEY SENT ME. I KNOW IT WILL MAKE THIS MORE DIFFICULT FOR YOU.
YING?!
TO BE CONTINUED!

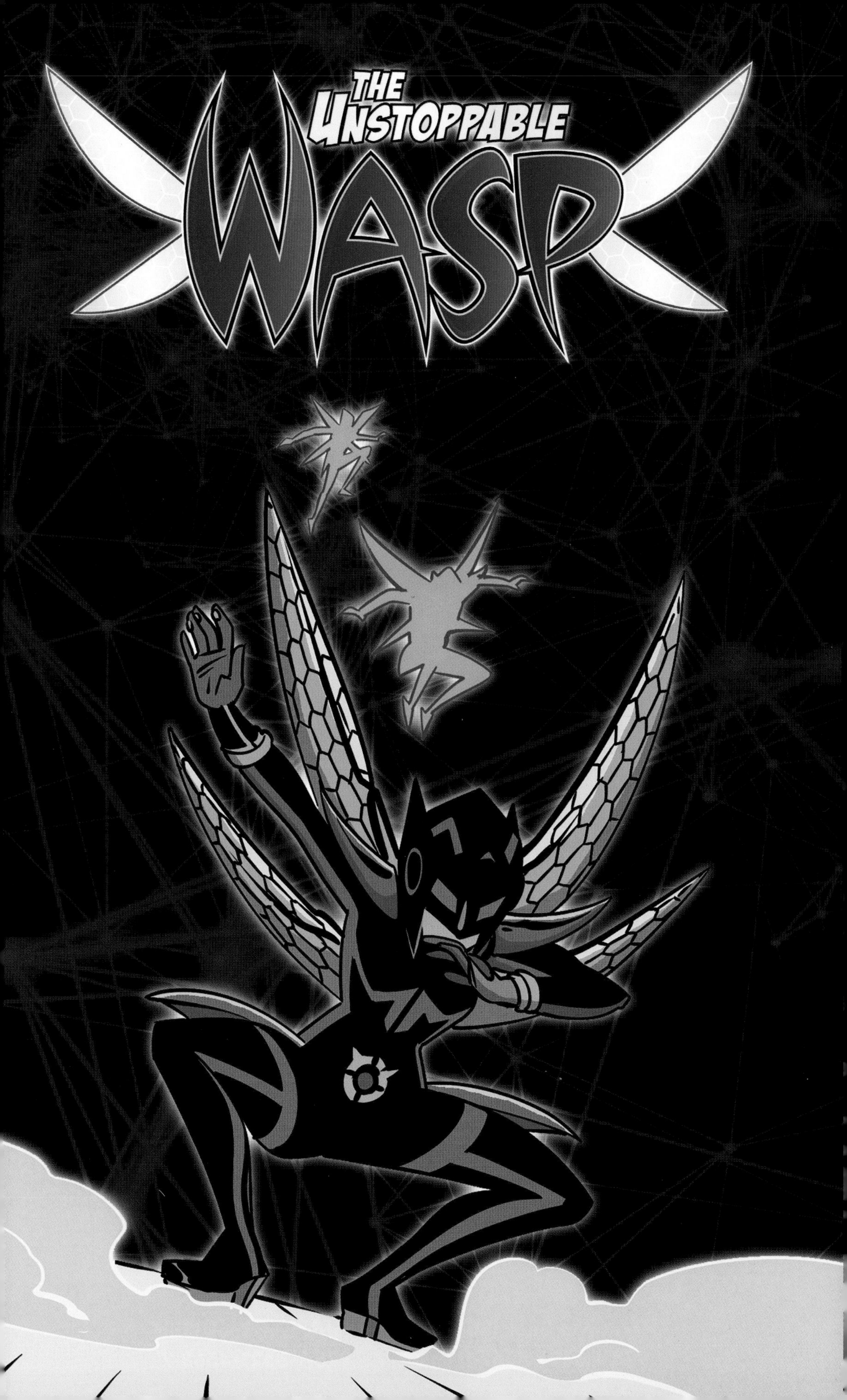
THE UNSTOPPABLE
WASP

THE UNSTOPPABLE WASP

COLLECT THEM ALL!

Set of 4 Hardcover Books ISBN: 978-1-5321-4364-9

THE UNSTOPPABLE WASP
UNSTOPPABLE! #1
MARVEL

Hardcover Book ISBN
978-1-5321-4365-6

THE UNSTOPPABLE WASP
GUEST-STARRING
MOON GIRL
UNSTOPPABLE! #2
MARVEL

Hardcover Book ISBN
978-1-5321-4366-3

THE UNSTOPPABLE WASP
FEATURING MOON GIRL
DEVIL
UNSTOPPABLE! #3
MARVEL

Hardcover Book ISBN
978-1-5321-4367-0

THE UNSTOPPABLE WASP
UNSTOPPABLE! #4
MARVEL

Hardcover Book ISBN
978-1-5321-4368-7

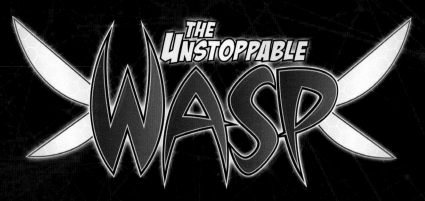

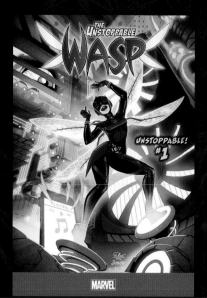

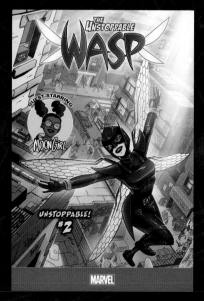

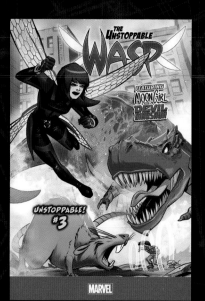

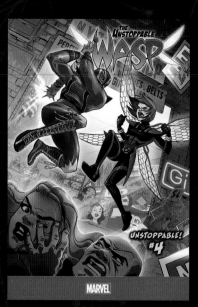